Anthropology

Anthropology

and a hundred other stories

Dan Rhodes

CANONGATE
Edinburgh · London

Thanks to: Tibor Fischer, Lawrence Norfolk, Sheenagh Pugh,
Tony Curtis, Stephen Knight, Christopher Meredith and, particularly,
W. B. & V. C. Rhodes.

This edition published in 2005 by
Canongate Books Ltd
14 High Street
Edinburgh EH1 1TE

This paperback edition published in 2010
by Canongate Books

First published in Great Britain in 2000 by
Fourth Estate
A Division of HarperCollins Publishers

2

A catalogue record for this book is available
from the British Library

ISBN 978 1 84195 614 5

Printed and bound in Great Britain by Clays Ltd, St Ives plc

www.canongate.tv

Contents

Anthropology

I loved an anthropologist. She went to Mongolia to study the gays. At first she kept their culture at arm's length, but eventually she decided that her fieldwork would benefit from assimilation. She worked hard to become as much like them as possible, and gradually she was accepted. After a while she ended our romance by letter. It breaks my heart to think of her herding those yaks in the freezing hills, the peak of her leather cap shielding her eyes from the driving wind, her wrist dangling away, and nothing but a handlebar moustache to keep her top lip warm.

Ashes

My girlfriend died. We hadn't been together long, and I had felt indifferent towards her. She left me her ashes. 'What should I do with them?' I asked her family.

'She wanted you to decide.' I really didn't care. 'You two were so in love; we're leaving it up to you to choose her final resting place.' They were incredibly compassionate, and the pressure was enormous. I found myself in a helicopter, scattering her over the meadow where she had ridden her pony as a girl. Her family watched, weeping their final goodbyes as the little grey flecks fell to earth.

Baby

My girlfriend's pregnancy lasted over two years. 'Maybe the doctor's right,' I said. 'Maybe a baby isn't going to come.' She wouldn't listen. She carried on buying nappies, teething rings, woolly hats and mittens, and little bits and pieces for the nursery. One afternoon I came home to find her cradling a bundle in her arms.

'Look,' she said. 'It's arrived. It's a boy, and it's got your eyes.'

'Well done,' I said. 'Congratulations.'

'And congratulations to you too. After all, you don't become a father every day.'

'I suppose not. But really it's you that's done all the hard work.'

Beauty

My girlfriend is so beautiful that she has never had cause to develop any kind of personality. People are always wildly glad to see her, even though she does little more than sit around and smoke. She's getting prettier, too. Last time she left the house she caused six car crashes, two coronaries, about thirty domestic disputes and an estimated six hundred unwanted and embarrassing erections. She seems to be quite indifferent to the havoc she causes. 'I'm going to the shop for cigarettes,' she'll say, yawning with that succulent, glossy mouth. 'I suppose you'd better call some ambulances or something.'

Binding

I found my girlfriend smashing our two-year-old's toes with a rock. I told her to stop. 'What are you doing?' I cried, above the baby's agonised wails.

'You wouldn't understand,' she said, winding a bandage tightly around the crushed digits. 'It's a woman thing. It'll help her get a boyfriend.'

'But darling, don't you remember what the doctor told us? It's a boy baby.'

'Really?' She looked surprised. 'Oh well. Men look nice with small feet too. I expect he'll be gay, anyway. He's got that look about him. See?' I had to agree that she had a point.

Blind

My girlfriend used my going blind as an excuse to start dressing sloppily. In the days when I could see her, she had always looked immaculate in the latest cuts of the best designer labels. Now, her high heels have been replaced by trainers, her silk stockings and short skirts by jeans, and her smart blouses and figure-hugging jackets by baggy jumpers. I haven't said anything yet, but it's getting to the point where I'm embarrassed to be seen with her as she gently holds my hand and guides me along, making sure I don't trip or bump into anything.

Bulletin

My girlfriend is so lovely that I can't help feeling sorry for all her ex-boyfriends. I'm sure they must spend all their time thinking about her and wondering what she could be up to. So every month I send them a bulletin detailing all the pretty things she has said and done. Sometimes I enclose a discarded pair of tights, or the stub of an eyebrow pencil. I feel I should do everything I can to make up for them having lost a girl with such soft brown hair, and whose feet are so small you can hardly see them.

Charging

My girlfriend started charging me for sex. She said she had to think of her future, and anyway her friends did it so why shouldn't she? I didn't mind too much because her basic rates were very reasonable, although she always expected tips for extras. Once, as she was holding the banknotes I'd given her up to the light to make sure they were real, I asked her if she ever went with anyone else for money. She was furious, and asked what kind of girl I thought she was. I said one with laughing eyes, and lovely long dark hair.

Chemicals

Unable to accept that Celestia was no more than a haphazard cluster of chemicals brought together by chance in a universe out of control, I started to believe. To give thanks for her pretty face and endearing ways, I've started getting up early and taking her from door to door, with a sign around her neck that asks: Am I just chemicals? 'Look at her,' I say to the bleary-eyed householders, 'and draw your own conclusion.'

Sometimes they chase us away, but usually they just mumble, 'She looks like chemicals to me,' and shut the door loudly in our faces.

Clever

Tabitha was declared a genius, and decided she needed more intellectual stimulation than I could provide. After weeks of searching, she found someone and brought him home. He looked far too handsome to be clever, but using words I could barely understand he told me I was history. The ravenous way Tabitha was kissing him suggested he had a point. She left me. For months I've lived in the hope of him being a useless lover, but yesterday she sent a fax telling me how much more accomplished he is than me at licking, fondling and many other matters of intimacy.

Club

Lulula got together with my friends' girlfriends, and formed what they called 'The Girlfriend Club'. They met regularly, and enjoyed themselves. We were delighted for them to be having so much fun, but were curious about what they got up to. They wouldn't tell us. Then one of the girls confessed in her sleep that these evenings were spent giggling, and looking at photographs of handsome, well-dressed men. Heartbroken, we implored them to disband. They wouldn't. Nowadays, whenever they get together we do as well, silently looking at pictures of their pretty faces as tears well up in our eyes.

Coping

My girlfriend left me, and I'm coping very well. Sometimes it's almost as though she hadn't run off with another man, and that she's still here with me. During the day I cope by imagining she's gone to the shop for some cheap cigarettes, and will be back at any moment, smiling with those lovely painted lips. When the shop's shut, I cope by telling myself that my favourite picture of her is real. I spend my evenings at the piano, singing love songs to her photographed face, and occasionally licking the black keys because they remind me of her skin.

Crying

My girlfriend left me, and I started crying in my sleep. My nightly lament became so loud that my neighbours called the police. The press found out, and people came to stand outside my house to hear me call her name and moan. Television crews arrived, and soon a search was on to find the object of my misery. They tracked her to her new boyfriend's house. I watched the coverage. People were saying they had expected her to be much more beautiful than she was, and that I should pull myself together and stop crying over such an ordinary girl.

Drawing

Paris had her bicycle stolen, and was never the same again. I try to visit her every month. Usually she is drawing intently, crayon on paper, confused crisscrossing lines which resemble nothing I have ever seen. 'That's lovely, Paris,' I tell her. 'What is it?'

'It's a bicycle.' Her pretty face lights up, and I remember why I fell in love with her. Then she looks away. 'I had one once.' She starts rocking slowly back and forth, tears streaming down her cheeks. I kiss her forehead, and return to my new love, who is aware of the situation and understands.

Drinking

I asked my girlfriend if she'd started drinking again. She said no. I searched her flat and found six empty three-litre bottles of White Lightning cider. 7.5%. When we met for lunch I showed them to her. 'What are these?'

'I don't know.'

'You must know. They were in your flat.'

She stalled. 'I didn't drink them.'

'Then who did?'

'No one. I used it as make-up remover.'

'All eighteen litres?'

'Yes.' She was wearing lipstick, and had mascara on the lashes of those innocent eyes. I told her she didn't need it; that she was pretty enough already.

Dust

Xanthe left me. I found out her new address, and returned the kettle she had left behind. The next day I took her a book she had lent me. I found a box of hairgrips, and delivered one each day. If she wasn't home I would post it with a long letter explaining how I had found it on the floor. When I had returned them all, I took her, on the tip of my finger, a tiny ball of dust. 'I remember seeing it fall from your dress one afternoon,' I said. 'The pretty one, with the flowers on it.'

Endless

Often, one or other of Foxglove's ex-boyfriends will turn up on our doorstep bearing expensive eye-shadow. 'Will you give her this?' they choke. 'It's her favourite shade.' I take it. Then, heartbroken, they lash out. 'She'll leave you,' they cry, fists flailing. 'She thinks I'm the handsomest man in the world. She told me once, when we were kissing.' I hurt them as little as possible, but always make sure I win the fight. Sometimes, cigarette in hand, she'll come out to watch, smouldering as those perfect, endless legs vanish into the hem of her tiny brown suede skirt.

Expecting

With her long blonde hair, lily-white skin and Cupid's bow lips, Mariedel looks like an angel. Naturally I was delighted when she fell pregnant, but the baby's slanty eyes suggested she had been unfaithful to me. She apologised, and I forgave her. Soon the pretty thing was expecting again, and this child was nut brown. I didn't say a word. With the little mulatto cradled in her arms she looked so lovely that I just couldn't risk losing her. 'At last,' I said, 'a little baby of our own,' and one kiss from that perfect mouth made everything right again.

Exploring

I arrived at Zazie's deathbed to find her kissing her best friend's lips, and playing with her breasts. There was an awkward silence, then: 'I've always wanted to try it and I'm running out of time, so . . .' Neither girl could look me in the eye. 'She said she'd let me, and . . .'

'Well? Did you enjoy it?' I had to know. They looked uncomfortable. Then Zazie lifted her hand to her friend's face, and smiled. They giggled, and started exploring each other's bodies. I felt like an intruder. As, weeping, I left, her death rattle shook the room. I didn't look back.

Faithful

My girlfriend died. I was heartbroken, and vowed to remain faithful to her memory. At first I had no difficulty; my distress was so great that I couldn't even contemplate kissing anyone else. But, after a while, another girl started showing an interest. I resisted her advances. 'You're very pretty,' I told her, 'but it's just too soon. I'm sorry.' She wouldn't give up. She kept gently touching me, and fluttering her mascara-coated eyelashes. Eventually I yielded, and fell into her arms. The man asked us to leave. He said our rustling, slurping and giggling was upsetting the other mourners.

Features

Jealous of couples with pet names for each other, we decided to think up our own. We racked our brains. Eventually, she came up with the name 'Femur' for me, after a childhood accident about which I had many stories. I settled on 'Girlfriend-features' because I couldn't think of anything else. Now, when we're with friends, we use our new names, and reprimand each other for doing so. 'Don't call me that when there are people around,' I say. 'Are you listening to me, Girlfriend-features?' She gives me one of her looks, but can't help breaking into a smile.

Flowers

Tallulah lost control of her gambling habit. We lost our home, and started living in a tent. She still couldn't stop. To settle an argument with someone, she staked her waist-length blonde hair on a bet about the loveliness of the flowers in the park. The tension was too much to bear, but she won. The flowers were exactly as lovely as she had said. She showed me her prize. It was the loser's hair, in an old pipe-tobacco tin. It was short, grey and flecked with dandruff. It looked greasy, and neither of us wanted to touch it.

Fun

My girlfriend started teasing me. At first I didn't mind her puffing out her cheeks to draw attention to my slight weight problem, or drawing pictures of my long-nosed profile on dusty vans. These days, as we walk along a crowded street, she will often joke in a loud voice about the frequency with which I find myself unable to bring her to pleasure, and how handsome other men are compared to me. People snigger behind their hands, and I try my hardest to laugh along. I don't want it to look as though I've got no sense of fun.

Glass

Tortoiseshell was sent to prison, and I went to visit her. I asked what she'd done wrong. She told me she'd been seen having sex in the street. 'That's funny, Tortoiseshell,' I said. 'I don't remember us doing that.'

'No, you wouldn't . . . I was with somebody else.' I was shocked, and she looked guilty. 'Do you forgive me?' she asked, looking terrific in her prison uniform, and pleading with her lovely heart-shaped face.

'Of course I forgive you,' I said. As my lips flew towards her, I broke my nose on the glass screen between us. She roared with laughter.

Groping

I invited my ex-girlfriend to the pictures, just as friends, and she said yes. During a particularly steamy kissing scene I couldn't resist taking a trip down Memory Lane by gently running my hand up and down the inside of her soft, bare leg. She ran screaming from the building. After the film I arrived home to find the police there, waiting to arrest me. I asked them why, and they told me I'd been accused of a groping offence. 'She never used to call it that,' I sobbed, trembling as they handcuffed me and led me to their van.

Herself

Running Water left me. She told me she was very fond of me, but that she needed some time to herself. Six weeks later I saw her outside the local church, wearing her very best ceremonial head-dress and clinging to the arm of an unusually handsome man. I rushed through the confetti, and glared at her. 'So how did you enjoy all that time to yourself?' I hissed.

'It was great, thanks,' she answered, smiling for the cameras, and looking even prettier than I remembered. 'I had two cups of coffee and a croissant, and then I read a magazine.'

History

As part of the getting-to-know-me process, Nightjar told me all about her ex-boyfriends. She went through her shoebox full of photographs. 'His penis was much bigger than yours,' she would say, 'but he had bad breath.' Or, 'He was quite old but he could still go all night.' When, at last, she had finished, she asked me about my romantic history. I told her I had been waiting all my life for that special someone, and how glad I was now I had finally found her. 'Ah. I see.' She rolled her eyes. 'You're one of those.'

Hobbies

My girlfriend had been unemployed for ages, so I was delighted when she finally applied for a job. She filled in the form in her best handwriting, but got stuck when they asked her to list all her hobbies. 'I've put smoking,' she said, 'but I can't think of anything else.' I racked my brains, but couldn't think of anything either.

'Well,' I said eventually, 'you could put sex. You enjoy making love to me, don't you?'

'No,' she said, chewing her pen. 'Not any more. I'll put hill walking. It's not as if they're going to check up on me.'

Honest

January said it was important for couples to be completely honest with each other, and I agreed. I told her very honestly how much time I spent thinking about her, that whenever I pictured the future she was always there by my side, and how even after three years together I sometimes couldn't help feeling a little nervous when she was around. She told me to stop. 'That wasn't what I meant,' she said. 'I meant I just don't love you any more.' She looked away. 'And the more I think about it, the more I realise I never really did.'

Indifference

Not wanting the intensity of my love to drive Skylark away, I feigned indifference. I worried that this tactic wasn't working; seeming bored in my company, she would keep looking at her watch as though impatient to go somewhere far better. Even so, we would always disinterestedly arrange to meet up again. When, besotted, I casually suggested we get married, she shrugged her shoulders and, yawning, said, 'Whatever.' I couldn't believe my luck. The man asked us whether we were prepared to love and cherish one another forever. Skylark said she might as well, and I told him I supposed so.

Innocence

I thought my beautiful fiancée was innocence itself until I met her parrot. She had taught it to say terrible things. Wank. Minge. Fist fuck. Stick it up your Jap's eye. I was disillusioned to find she had taken such delight in training an unknowing bird to swear. My love diminished, but I didn't cancel the wedding. The parrot was in the church. When the man asked whether anyone knew a reason for us not to marry, it squawked, 'Cunt flaps.' My bride bent double with laughter, and even though we made our vows I knew that the marriage was over.

Kangaroo

Every day I find a new way of telling Tadhana how much I love her. I used to worry that she didn't believe me, so one evening she came home from work to find me wired to a lie-detector machine. Very sincerely, I told her just how much I cared for her, and how pleased I was with the way our relationship was going. This was verified by a series of bleeps. Today I gave her a life-size cuddly kangaroo. When she squeezes it, she activates a recording of my voice, crying: 'Please don't ever leave me. Please stay.'

Kiss

Orchid is resolute that her first kiss be perfect. I took her to Paris in the Springtime. As we gazed across the Seine at the Eiffel Tower, I made my move. She pushed me away. 'No,' she said. 'It's just not romantic enough. I'm sorry.' I took her to a deserted, palm-fringed Bahamian beach, and her response was the same. I saved and saved until finally we stood at sunset before the Taj Mahal. 'It smells funny,' she said. 'It smells, and there's poor people everywhere.' I was disappointed too. The supposedly magnificent structure paled beside those untouched, velvet lips.

Kissing

Since the moment we met, my wife and I have not stopped kissing. I'm Catholic and she's Islamic, so there were complications. Throughout the delicate negotiations with our families, our lips did not part for a moment. Eventually they accepted our love, so we married. We walked, tongues tangled, down the aisle. Now, after six years of marriage, we are still fused. We had our first child without stopping kissing for the conception, pregnancy or birth. Our lips are four broken scabs, and our chins always covered in blood, but we will never stop. We are far too much in love.

Knife

I gave Lola a knife to use in the kitchen. Instead she had a lump of oak delivered, and began to carve. For days I couldn't work out what it would be, and she wouldn't tell me. She barely spoke, so intent was she on the task. It took shape. It was a man: taller, more handsome and far better endowed than me. She tells me she still loves me and that she knows he isn't real, but sometimes, as her long nails scratch my back and her white teeth gnaw my body, I swear I can hear her whisper 'Woody'.

Laughing

My girlfriend died laughing at one of my funny faces. Her friends were kind, and told me I shouldn't feel guilty; that she would have wanted to have died that way. They weren't there as her musical laughter turned to chokes, grunts and her death rattle. When I stopped grieving I found a beautiful new girl to love. She died laughing at a joke I made about her feet. The next one passed away similarly. My last girlfriend didn't die. She left me. She said we never had any fun together, that she wanted a man with a sense of humour.

Leaving

Badr-al-Budur told me she was leaving. The idea of either of us walking out on such a perfect romance was so funny I started to laugh. 'That's a good one,' I said, clutching my sides. 'You really had me going there, Badr-al-Budur.'

'No,' she said. 'I mean it. I'm really leaving. I'm sorry.' She grabbed her holdall, and rushed out of the house.

'Don't go,' I called after her, bending double and expecting her to scurry straight back in, smiling like a mischievous little pixie and dashing over to help me dry my eyes, which had filled with tears of laughter.

Lesbian

My girlfriend and I couldn't decide on a name for our little baby girl. Eventually she took her to the registrar, and said she would think of something on the way. When she returned, I was frantic with anticipation. 'So what's she called?'

'I called her Lesbian,' she said, smiling at the bundle in her arms. 'It's such a pretty name.'

I asked her what on earth had possessed her. 'Don't you know what it means?' She didn't, so I explained. The poor thing burst into tears.

'I didn't know there were ladies who did that to each other,' she sobbed.

Lilac

I was overcome with the desire to build. I bought bricks and cement and started work, going as high as I could. The tower was a little lopsided, and I tried to disguise this with thick layers of plaster. I painted it lilac, her favourite colour, as well as her name. I had not thought to dig deep foundations, and the clumsy oblong toppled in an autumn gale. These days it lies on my lawn, a haphazard pile of masonry. Hardly an appropriate tribute to one with such pretty lips, and whose kisses were so warm I can still feel them.

Lipstick

The police caught my girlfriend stealing money from a blind beggar. She kept silent, but they tortured her until she admitted that she needed it for lipstick. 'You have a job,' they barked. 'You can afford lipstick.'

'I can afford cheap lipstick, but it's horrible. It's soapy, and it never lasts.'

Fortunately, one of her interrogators was a woman. 'She's right. A girl needs to feel confident about her cosmetics.' They gave her a caution. As they released her the female officer, overcome with pity, slipped something into my girlfriend's pocket. A stick of Lancôme. Volcanique. It suits her very well.

Lost

My girlfriend was lost in space, and I was at my wits' end. Eventually her spaceship was located and brought down to Earth. I was euphoric. She was full of stories of how frightened she was when her circuit died, and how incredible it was to be in orbit. It was wonderful to hear, but she has been back for some time now and I wish she would change the subject. This morning she told me again that the Earth was about the size of a tennis ball, and the moon seemed much bigger and brighter than it ever had before.

Madrid

I was delighted to find a Spanish girlfriend, and celebrated our first anniversary with a surprise trip to her home city. I landed our helicopter in front of the Palacio Real, and took off her blindfold. 'Where is this?' she asked, in her lilting Iberian accent. I was surprised that she didn't recognise such a famous landmark, and suggested she ask a passer-by. She started crying. In a voice I didn't recognise, she told me she was sorry, that there had been a special offer on sunbeds, and it had seemed like the right thing to say at the time.

Milestones

My girlfriend left me. I found she had been seeing lots of other men all along. She was loose, and I thought the world should know. I calculated the road distances from her house to over two thousand different locations around the country, and began to carve milestones. 'Mette's open legs: 263km.' That was the first one. I laid it on a verge just outside Ulfborg. After I had planted nine hundred and forty, I realised that it was not making me any happier, that I was carving them in heart-shapes, and that I missed her like nothing on earth.

Money

My girlfriend had always enjoyed showing off in front of foreigners, and when we met a Greek in a restaurant she swung from the ceiling fan. Amused, he increased its speed and she flew off, cracking her head on the floor. The Greek felt he should accept responsibility for her passing, and tries hard to compensate for my having lost such a lovely girl. Every month he sends drachmas or gold. My new wife feels funny about it, but that doesn't stop her spending it all on pretty dresses and paint for her face. She calls it her dead girl money.

Museum

I turned our flat into a museum. Visitors are welcome to marvel at the daintiness of the pumps she left behind, and to look at the band with which she would tie her hair back from the face I kissed so many times. There are cabinets full of photographs, and letters she sent me. There's a framed birthday card on the wall, with three big kisses in silver pen. No one ever visits but I'm here every day, keeping my head as still as I can. I don't want to lose any of the brain cells that hold those precious memories.

Naked

Phuong's parachute failed to open, but she survived against all the odds. I visited her in hospital. She was entirely encased in plaster, except for her mouth. I asked her what had gone through her mind as she fell helpless towards the ground. Gently, she told me she had not given me a second thought; that she had only seen the face of her favourite radio star. Weeping, I asked her if there was anything I could do before leaving her life forever. She asked me to apply some expensive lipstick to her lips. She said she felt naked without it.

Nature

Amber suddenly discovered naturism. We went to the supermarket, and people couldn't help staring at her. She's very pretty, and the security guards were too shy to ask her to cover herself up. 'Darling,' I whispered, 'people are looking.'

'Let them,' she replied. 'I've got nothing to be ashamed of.' She told me she would leave me there and then if I didn't join her and stop wearing clothes. 'It goes against nature,' she explained. I took off my trousers, and the shoppers jeered at my skinny legs. When, at last, I took off my underpants they waggled their little fingers.

Noises

My girlfriend had been unemployed for ages, but eventually she found some work in an office. Although I couldn't find the courage to say anything, I was worried that her new role in life would come between us. She's been there some time now, and although she spends most of her working day furtively ringing me up to make kissing noises, I can't help feeling as though she's slipping away from me. The slurps from the other end of the line don't seem as passionate as they could be. It's almost as if her lips had other things on their mind.

Open

Melody suggested we begin an open relationship. Petrified of losing her, I enthusiastically agreed. These days I spend most nights alone on the sofa as she uses our bed to entertain her new boyfriends and girlfriends with rubberwear, bondage, coprophilia and DIY exhibitionism. Sometimes she asks me how I am finding our new approach to life and love, and I tell her that I like it very much. I daren't say that sometimes, as the low moans of a threesome fly from the bedroom, I catch myself wishing things could be just a little bit more like the old days again.

Ouija

Aurélia's experiment with herbal contraception failed, and we started expecting a baby. We were both very excited, and she was so impatient to meet the future member of our family that she decided to make contact through a ouija board. Wary of such things, I stayed out of the way, but when she had finished I was consumed with curiosity. 'So did the baby spell anything?' I asked.

'Well,' she said. 'He said he was going to be a boy.'

'That's wonderful. Anything else?'

'Yes.' Overcome with joy she sighed, smiled and patted her bump. 'He said, "Mummy I love you."'

Paint

My girlfriend is so besotted that she can't take her eyes off me. After we've turned out the light she puts on her night-vision goggles, and watches me as I sleep. Quite often I am woken by her sighing and her involuntary yelps of happiness. This has been going on for years, and is showing no sign of abating. Once I asked her to stop all this infra-red activity, but it didn't really work; I'd wake up to find her covering me in luminous paint, and softly whispering, 'Sometimes I wonder if you know how much I love you.'

Pilot

My girlfriend had been unemployed for ages, so I was overjoyed when she found work as an airline pilot. She was excited, looked great in her cap and set off for Lisbon on her maiden flight. The silly thing was so busy fixing her lipstick in the rear-view mirror that she didn't notice her 747 heading straight for the Pyrenees. She ejected in time, but the passengers and crew perished. She lost the job, and is now back at home all day, eating cold baked beans with a knife, and trying to straighten her hair by pulling it really hard.

Plain

I've been seeing a plain girl for several years. Her mother enrolled in cosmetic surgery school, and we offered to help out. So, she's using my girlfriend as her final project, the idea being that she transforms her from a plain Jane into a textbook beauty. Now, when she walks around in obvious distress from her breast remodelling, black eyes peeping from her bandaged face, men approach her and give her their phone numbers. They are sure that when the swelling goes down she will look quite incredible. I hope her mother fails the course, that the project ends in disaster.

Pneumonia

My girlfriend started coughing. Unable to bear the thought of her dying and leaving me to face the world alone, I rushed her to hospital. I demanded that they put her on a life-support machine. 'Quickly,' I screamed. 'Before it's too late.' The doctor told me she wasn't slipping away, that all she had was a little cold. I couldn't believe him. Before long we were surrounded by medical personnel. Jeering, and shouting terrible words, they chased us away. 'But what if it's terminal pneumonia?' I yelled, as stethoscopes and scalpels bounced off our heads. 'What would I do then?'

Precious

My ex-girlfriend and her new husband regularly stand outside my house, kissing and smiling at each other. I love her so much that I cannot ignore them. Every opportunity to see her is precious, and I press my face against the window. Sometimes they break off from their love play to look, point and jeer at me. Often her husband makes terrible signs with his fingers while my ex-girlfriend bends double, laughing hysterically as the tears stream down my face. The days we spent together were the happiest of my life, and I will always, always want her back.

Proust

I came home to find her packing. I'd had no idea things had gone wrong between us. 'I've been reading,' she explained. '"A cathedral, a wave of a storm, a dancer's leap, never turn out to be as high as we had hoped." That's why I have to go.' She patted my arm. 'I'm sorry.'

'But don't forget,' I blurted, '"All our final resolutions are made in a state of mind which is not going to last."' I was clutching at straws, and she knew it. She folded her pretty red dress, zipped up her holdall, and went without another word.

Pumpkins

I told Sapphire I'd always wanted to grow pumpkins; that my dream was to grow one so big that I could hollow it out and sit in it. Then, if it was watertight, I would climb in and float down the river on carnival day, waving to the children on the shore. She broke off from painting her long nails to tell me I'd be lucky to grow a pumpkin big enough for a dog, let alone a person, and that even if I could there would be no point. I decided she was right. I don't want to grow pumpkins.

Rehearsing

Mazzy started acting. Having such a pleasing face, she is always cast as the female lead. She rehearses at home. While I'm in the armchair watching television she's often sprawled on the sofa, perfecting the crucial clinch with her leading man. She tells me that her little gasps and sighs of pleasure are in the script. When I saw her in the park, writhing mouth to mouth with another man, I was upset and told her as much. She was indignant: 'Do you mind? We're rehearsing.' They went back to their rehearsal and I walked away, ashamed at having doubted her.

Sailing

My girlfriend cannot play the guitar. She strums slowly, erratically and woefully out of time. She sucks her lips in concentration, and sometimes stalls for as many as fifteen seconds between chord changes. When she stops playing, her eyes are bright with anticipation. 'OK. What was that?'

'I'm not sure. Was it "Moon River"?'

'No.' She looks disappointed. 'It was "We Are Sailing". You know, by Paul McCartney.' She starts another, and I know I won't be able to identify it, no matter how hard I try. This has been going on for seven perfect years. I hope she never learns.

Salesman

Tammy is a successful travelling salesman. Her job takes her away an awful lot, but I don't complain for fear of losing her. When she leaves she always looks very attractive in short, tight dresses and crimson lipstick. Often she's gone for days on end, and is too busy to call. I wish she would change her job. I'd like us to get married, and for her not to have to be away nearly so much. The lifestyle is bad for her. The hours are far too long, and she keeps catching venereal diseases from the toilet seats of faraway towns.

Saving

'I gotta go score,' my girlfriend would say at three or four a.m. She would return hours later, considerably out of pocket. She seemed healthy enough. Her eyes still sparkled and her cheeks glowed. 'You look well,' I would say.

'Thank you. I know.'

I told her I wanted an addiction too. 'We're a couple. We should do things together.' I pestered her until finally she confessed to never having taken heroin in her life. She wouldn't tell me anything else, but I looked everywhere and eventually found the money. She'd stitched it into the mattress, like a crazy old woman.

Schnauzer

For weeks I looked forward to our first Valentine's Day together, and could think of little else. When, at last, the special day arrived, she told me she'd been doing a lot of thinking, and had decided that it would be best for both of us if we were to go our separate ways. I was heartbroken, but I just had to give her all the gifts I'd spent so long preparing: red roses, champagne, perfume, Swiss chocolates, five gold rings and a schnauzer with a big pink ribbon around it. I'd been dying to see her little face light up.

Shipwreck

After the shipwreck I was devastated and cried for weeks. When I emerged from my grief I realised that my girlfriend's death shouldn't be the end of me. I found someone as pretty and nice as her, and eventually I invited her on a beach holiday. My old girlfriend was washed up on the shore. She'd been clinging to a plank for fourteen months, living on raw fish, rainwater and her love for me. I was faced with a choice. My new girl won because the old one was skinny and bedraggled, and besides, the water had made her all crinkly.

Shivers

My girlfriend is so in love with me I can hardly bear it. She's always telling me how manly my hands are, how attractive she finds my brow, and that the sound of my voice sends shivers right through her. Once, I tried to change the subject. 'Can we talk about something else for a change?' I asked.

'Of course we can't,' she said. 'How do you expect me to concentrate on anything else when you're there with your white teeth?' I closed my eyes and shook my head. 'Oh, do that again,' she cried. 'It makes you look so handsome.'

Snakes

On returning from the Far East, my girlfriend decided to crouch on the pavement of the high street, selling terrapins and snakes. Trade was brisk, but she found herself in an awkward spot when a hungry python ate a passing child. The child's father was livid, and thrashed her so hard that she lost her sight. I hoped this would make her abandon her Oriental ways and settle into a more conventional lifestyle. Instead she reclaimed her old spot on the pavement, where she squats to this day, bellowing tuneless songs into an ancient microphone and hoping for low-denomination notes.

Special

My beautiful girlfriend and I are so at ease with our relationship that we feel perfectly happy to hold hands and kiss in public. When we see a person who looks a little lonely, we'll walk past them with our arms around each other, gazing contentedly into each other's eyes. If they don't notice us at first, we'll go back and stand directly in front of them, kissing passionately, sighing, and touching each other's bodies in the way only lovers can. It's so important for these people to see just how perfect life can be once you've found that special someone.

Squeals

Within minutes of meeting my fiancée I realised we were incompatible, but by then there was no turning back. So delighted to have met me, she immediately started making wedding preparations. I tried to think of a way of telling her it would never work, that I could never love her, but my mind went blank. Carried away by the moment she kept smiling at me, sighing, patting my hand and excitedly biting her lip. Delirious, she called her mother to tell her the good news. She told her I was Taurean, and I could hear the maternal squeals of delight.

Straight

When we started seeing each other, Miracle told me it was no big deal, that we were just friends who happened to be spending some time as lovers. Eventually, though, we moved in together and started a family. Seven years and three beautiful children later, she suddenly announced that she was leaving, that she had found somebody new. Between sobs I told her I felt let down and betrayed.

'Oh, come on,' she snapped, rolling those lovely, limpid eyes and shaking her head in disbelief. 'Don't give me all that. Are you seriously trying to say I wasn't straight with you?'

Stuff

Treasure left me. 'I'm so sorry,' she said. 'I understand how awful you must feel.' Choking, I told her she couldn't begin to understand. She insisted that she could. 'You know you'll never find anyone as pretty as me,' she explained, 'or as nice, and your every moment will be clouded by nagging recollections of times we spent together; times when you wrongly believed we had some kind of future. Believe me, I understand,' she said, gently. 'A part of you has died, the part capable of loving and trusting, and you know you'll never get it back. Stuff like that.'

Support

Tired of her ex-boyfriends desperately trying to get back with her, my girlfriend arranged a support group for them. When she told me she loved me very much, but only as a friend, she gave me their number and I went along. We meet every week. Sitting in a big circle, we try to get over her by talking about other things. It isn't easy. Every subject we try seems to return to the warmth of her naked body beside us in the morning, or the way she flicks her hair away from her face as she smokes a cigarette.

Sushi

My town has a university, so for nine months of the year there are pretty Japanese girls everywhere. I like to watch them as they walk around. With their little smiling faces and shiny black hair, they seem like such nice people. There's one that's my favourite, and every time I see her I approach her and ask for a quick language lesson, or ask her whether she knows a good place to eat sushi. So far I have learned all the numbers up to twenty-three, and been told several times that the nearest Japanese restaurant is some way away.

Tagged

When we started getting serious, I had my girlfriend electronically tagged. She thought this was terribly romantic, and whenever my radar device brought me to her work, the park, a café or a friend's house, she greeted me with a delighted smile and a long, gentle kiss. Lately I've started to worry that she's unwell. When I track her to the pool or the train she appears less surprised, her smile lacks its former dazzle, and her kisses leave my cheek much sooner than before. She seems distant and thoughtful. She really isn't herself. I think she should see a doctor.

Taxidermy

Columbine broke her neck by mistake. I took her to the taxidermist, and they delivered to my house a fortnight later. When I unwrapped the package I found the wrong girl. I reached for the telephone, but something stopped me. I looked again. The girl was pretty. Her hair was longer than Columbine's; her cheekbones more regal. I placed her in the diorama I had already prepared. Her boyfriend found out and came round for her, but I gave him some money and he went away. He told me she had been Australian, and that he had never really liked her.

Together

Hummingbird is the answer to my prayers. We spend our evenings kissing and gently stroking each other's skin, but this idyll is always shattered by a phone call from one ex-boyfriend or another. In mortified chokes they tell her how much they still love her, and how unbearable the pain is, sometimes even several years after the break-up. Hysterical, they beg for her to take them back. She listens politely, tells them to pull themselves together, and puts the phone down. 'That'll be you one day,' she purrs, and kisses me so sweetly that it almost breaks my heart.

Toys

On the last day of our relationship, my girlfriend brought toys. I had no idea our romance had ended, and was delighted to join her in a Connect 4 contest. 'It's over,' she told me, halfway through a game.

'What's over?' I asked, happy to be having so much fun.

'You and me,' she replied, abandoning Connect 4 and plugging in Astro Wars. 'I don't want to see you any more.' I tried to see how much she was scoring, but was blinded by tears. I knew the game, and just by listening I could tell she was doing very well.

Tractor

My girlfriend waited until I'd finished fixing her tractor before telling me we had no future together. I was knocked for six, and begged for an opportunity to talk things over. She told me she had made up her mind, and that nothing I could say would change it. I continued to plead, but she just put on her ear-muffs and drove away. I called after her, my voice hoarse with emotion, 'Think of all the happy times we've spent together.' I don't think she heard me. She just kept on driving, her golden hair glowing in the evening light.

Trick

My girlfriend told me she had been the victim of nature's cruellest trick, that although born male she had always felt female. She said she had started dressing in women's clothes at the age of seventeen, and three years later had undergone the necessary surgery. I was stunned, but told her that I loved her first and foremost as a person, and that I would give her all the emotional support she needed. She looked horrified. She had only been joking. She left me. She said she was going to find a real man, not some queer little gayboy like me.

Trouble

My girlfriend and I have been sharing a flat for several months. Most mornings she asks me whether I would like something to drink. 'We've got tea or coffee,' she says.

'I'm fine,' I say. 'Really.'

'But it's no trouble. I'll be having something myself. Which would you prefer?' I tell her I prefer coffee, but that I'm really not thirsty. 'But you've got to have something before you go to work,' she insists, looking intently at the kettle.

'OK, I'll have a coffee,' I say reluctantly, my body screaming out for caffeine. 'But only if it's not too much trouble.'

Truncheon

My girlfriend joined the police without telling me. I didn't find out for two years, and then I came across a truncheon in the magazine rack. Confronted with this evidence she blushed, stammered and looked so pretty that I forgave her. She put on her uniform, and it was like falling in love all over again. I kissed her, and she kissed me. Together we walked into the bedroom. I began to undress. The moment I took down my underpants she arrested me for indecent exposure. She gave evidence against me in court, and I served six months. She didn't visit.

Video

After Firefly left me I presented her with a video recording I had made of myself, so if she ever felt down she could be reminded that there was somebody out there who loved her more than anything in the world. I met her in the street, and asked her if she ever watched it. She said she did, and that it always cheered her up. She told me she particularly liked the part where I kissed and caressed the tiny black skirt she had left behind, and cried like a new-born baby. She said that always made her smile.

Violins

Petrified at the thought of age withering my boyish good looks, Sundial blinded herself with a soldering iron. 'You're handsome today,' she tells me every morning, dark glasses hiding the mess in her sockets. 'Every time I'm near you I hear violins.'

'But how do you know I'm so handsome, Sundial?' I ask, as I pat her hand and run my fingers through her hair. 'You can't see me any more.'

'Oh, I just know you are. It must be those violins. Sometimes I wish they'd shut up.' She flashes me an impish smile, so I know she doesn't mean it.

Volcano

The volcano erupted. Wanting our love to be preserved forever, we stood outside and started kissing. Everyone else fled for cover, but not us; we wanted to be petrified by the ash, so future generations could visit us and see how special we were to each other. However, the volcano wasn't as destructive as everyone had anticipated, and we survived with extensive burns. Even so, people come to look at us, and to marvel at our devotion. They ask us to kiss for them. They take photographs, as the reptilian moonscapes where our faces used to be join together in love.

Words

I fell in love the moment I saw her in her grandfather's kitchen, her dark curls crashing over her Portuguese shoulders. 'Would you like to drink coffee?' she smiled.

'I'm really not that thirsty.'

'What? What you say?' Her English wasn't too good. Now I'm seventy-three and she's just turned seventy. 'Would you like to drink coffee?' she asked me today, smiling.

'I'm really not that thirsty.'

'What? What you say?' Neither of us has the gift of language acquisition. After fifty years of marriage we have never really spoken, but we love each other more than words can say.

LITTLE HANDS CLAPPING

DAN RHODES

The following pages contain an extract from *Little Hands Clapping*, Dan Rhodes's exciting new novel.

In a room above a bizarre German museum, far from the prying eyes of strangers, lives the Old Man. Caretaker of the museum by day, by night he enjoys nothing more than the sound of silence, broken only by the occasional crunch of a spider between his teeth.

Little Hands Clapping brings the Old Man together with the respectable Doctor Ernst Fröhlicher, his loveable dog Hans and a cast of grotesque and hilarious townsfolk, who all become entwined in a crime so outrageous it will shock the world.

From its sinister opening to its explosive denouement, *Little Hands Clapping* blends lavishly entertaining storytelling with Rhodes's macabre imagination, entrancing originality and magical touch.

'Reliably odd but fabulous.' *Guardian*

'My favourite author who isn't dead.'
STEWART LEE

'Rhodes is that real, rare thing – a natural storyteller.' *Sunday Times*

£7.99

ISBN 978 1 84767 530 9

www.canongate.tv

I

At night, indeed at any time, but most of all at night, when the narrow street is lit only by the occasional lamp, there is little to distinguish the museum from the other buildings in the old part of the city. It is painted white, and rises three stories before tapering into a roof, where small windows jut from the immaculate tiles. It is set apart from its neighbours by the brass plate beside the door, which gives, in four languages, its name and the hours when its contents can be viewed. Only by standing close and squinting into the darkness is it possible to read the lettering, and as the first warm day of the year nears its end, nobody is taking the time to squint into the darkness. A small party of tourists passes by without paying the place any attention. They turn a corner, their voices fade, and the street is quiet until the next group comes along, young locals this time, their after-work drink having turned into a meal and several more drinks, their conversation reverberating from the high buildings as they head to somebody's apartment for a final glass.

The museum's lights are off, but that is not to say that the place is unoccupied. Behind one of the small windows sleeps an old man in a nightshirt and nightcap, their whiteness incandescent as it cuts through the dark. Partly covered by a single white sheet, and oblivious to the bursts of activity from the street below, he lies on a narrow bed. The skin of his face, a faint grey against the cotton that encases him, is a mosaic of oblongs, triangles and shapes without names. His mouth is open, his eyes are closed and the rattle of his breath fills the room. The old man is the museum's only resident, but this night he is not alone. The visitors are supposed to leave by five o'clock, but one had stayed on, huddling behind a large wooden display board as the door was bolted shut, and building up the courage to do what they had been meaning to do for so long. There are no sobs to be heard, and no wails. The visitor feels calm, and ready at last.

When this business is over and the story is out, or as much of the story as will ever be out, such interlopers will be described as having been drawn to the place *like moths to a flame*. While they are being counted and identified, articles will be written; some sober and balanced, others gleefully bug-eyed. None will capture the essence of the old man or even get a real grip on the events that had taken place under this roof. Nor will they convey any more than the haziest sense of the lives of these supposed moths, at least not what will often be referred to as their *inner lives* – the details beyond their education, employment history and haphazard lists of their likes and dislikes. With so little known about the thoughts and feelings from which they were built, these people will be presented to the world as having amounted to little more than a curriculum vitae, or a lonely hearts advertisement.

The more ambitious reporters will attempt to write something reflective, but frustrated by the incalculable blank spaces they will find their prose leaning towards the overwrought as they try, without much success, to make their way beneath the surface of the story. Their interviews with acknowledged experts will add nothing of interest to the copy, and references to Othello and Ophelia, Haemon and Antigone and the works of Émile Durkheim and David Hume will make them appear not so much learned as desperate. It is the tabloid writers who will be happiest, seasoning the facts with amateur psychological profiling, coarse conjecture and simple, alliterative blasts of moral condemnation as they pull together lurid account after lurid account.

Not wanting to know much beyond the basics,

most people will only read around the edges of these articles. Looking at the photographs they will begin, but no more, to imagine what must have been happening behind the eyes that sometimes stare back at them, and sometimes scowl, but more often than not smile.

At no stage will an editor allow an article to reach the press unless somewhere the people such as the one huddling behind the large display board are described as having been *like moths to a flame*. But if this place is a flame, it is a cold one. Even on a night like this the warmth has not penetrated the thick walls, and a wintry chill still pervades the building.

The last drunk of the night passes in the street, singing a song from generations ago, learned in childhood and never forgotten:

> *Frieda, oh Frieda,*
> *Will you still be mine*
> *When I am back from the war*
> *With a patch on my eye?*

It is supposed to be sung as a duet, but the drunk takes the woman's part too, a squawking, quavering parody of the female voice as she tells him that yes, of course she will still love him even though he has lost an eye.

Frieda, oh Frieda,
Will you still be mine
When I am back from the
War with my left arm torn off to the shoulder?

The shrieking Frieda tells him again that she will still love him, at which point he reveals yet another body part lost on the battlefield. Just as Frieda is telling him she will still love him in spite of his right foot having been amputated after becoming gangrenous in a mantrap, the drunk takes a turning and the words become indistinct. Everybody who has heard him knows the song, and how it finishes: the soldier continues to break news to Frieda about further losses of body parts until there is almost nothing left for her to love, and she tells him that she will still be his, no matter what. It is a simple song of true love – perhaps that is why it has remained so popular and why, even when sung by a drunk late at night, no reports are made of his antisocial behaviour.

The moth, huddling in the darkness, knows it to be a lie. But it is too late for anger. *Let them believe that if they want to. After all, they are only taking comfort, and who can blame them? For me, though, it is too late for comfort.* The voice fades, and fades, and soon it is gone altogether.

At ten past three the old man jolts awake at the sharp smack of wood on wood from one of the rooms below.

He sits up and listens for any further disturbance, but none occurs. He sets his alarm for five, then lies back and closes his eyes. He knows the sound, and that it can be dealt with later on. His mouth falls open, and once again his breathing fills the room, beginning as a light wheeze then escalating into a rattle, the inhalations and exhalations at a pitch so indistinguishable that it seems like a single undulating drone.

A fat house spider crawls across the sheet, clear against the bright white. It steps onto the sleeve of his nightshirt, where it lingers for a while before scuttling up to his neck. The moment the first of the eight dark brown legs touches the old man's cold skin he wakes once again. He does not move, but the rattle stops dead and his breathing becomes soft and shallow. The spider sprints to his cheek, where it remains still for a moment before moving towards his mouth. It stops again, as if considering its next move, and then, with an agility bordering on grace, it darts into the chasm.

The old man's mouth shuts and the spider races around, trying to make its way out, but there is no escape from the thin, grey tongue that pushes it first into his cheek and then between his back teeth. After some final desperate flailing, the spider is crunched into a gritty paste and the tongue moves around the old man's teeth, collecting stray pieces.

His breathing slows, and he swallows the final traces. Soon the rattle returns. In and out, in and out. It all sounds the same.

DON'T TELL ME THE TRUTH ABOUT LOVE

DAN RHODES

A chance encounter prompts an ageing profes-
sor to regret a lifetime of wasted opportunities;
a beautiful wife tests her husband by making
herself hideous; for the love of a girl, a boy
turns himself into a violoncello.

Funny, magical and strange, in these seven short
stories Dan Rhodes lays bare the pain and
enchantment of love.

'Often macabre, always musical, Rhodes flirts
with laugh-out-loud absurdity but stays in close
contact with pathos . . . his arch, askew take on
the heart's muddle flourishes.' *Uncut*

'The beauty of his writing is persuasive and his
themes are universal.' *The Times*

'Extremely readable – thought-provoking as
well as entertaining.'
Times Literary Supplement

£8.99

ISBN 978 1 84195 613 8

www.canongate.tv

TIMOLEON VIETA COME HOME

DAN RHODES

Winner of the Author's Club First Novel Award
Winner of the QPB New Voices Award
Shortlisted for Le Prince Maurice Prize
Shortlisted for the John Llewellyn Rhys Prize

Meet the mongrel: Timoleon Vieta, a deeply
loyal and loving companion, with the most
beautiful eyes. He is living an idyllic existence
in the Italian countryside with Cockroft, a
composer in exile. Until, that is, the
mysterious and malevolent 'Bosnian' comes to
stay. How will the stranger affect the bond
between dog and master?

'A delight, a masterpiece of beautifully unforced
comedy.' *Observer*

'Quirky and original, and the storytelling is
truly virtuoso. A literary treasure.'
LOUIS DE BERNIÈRES

'Charming, original, funny, biting and wise.'
Guardian

£7.99

ISBN 978 1 84767 562 0

www.canongate.tv

LITTLE WHITE CAR

DANUTA DE RHODES

After a relationship-breaking argument with her dull boyfriend, Veronique jumps into her little white Fiat and drives off into the Paris night.

Feeling the effects of the wine she has been drinking, she makes sure she drives slowly and carefully, down into the underpass, not wanting to hit the sides of the tunnel . . .

The Little White Car is a feel-good buddy novel about the untimely death of Diana, Princess of Wales, and how two gorgeous French girls go about urgently dismantling a car . . . while an enormous dog sniffs around in the garden.

'Fabulous . . . Perhaps Dan Rhodes thought that by rebranding himself as a lady novelist, we would sit up and take more notice. Well he's right! This is a very funny, very charming novel that we quite simply insist you read. Danuta is a very talented storyteller indeed.' *Heat*

'This is why French women dress better than we do: this book follows all the rules of finding the perfect pair of shoes. It's beautifully crafted, chic, witty, simultaneously classic and contemporary, and will stay with you forever.' Jenny Colgan, author of *Amanda's Wedding*.

£8.99

ISBN 978 1 84195 528 5

www.canongate.tv

GOLD

DAN RHODES

Miyuki Woodward, lover of pints and Pot Noodles, has been spending holidays in the same Welsh seaside town for years. She loves the wet walks, she loves The Anchor and most of all she loves the pub-quiz.

This year, following an act of raw creativity involving some cans of gold spray paint, Miyuki will take part in the most turbulent events the village has seen since Tall Mr Hughes returned from the pub toilet without remembering to button up.

'Hilarious and acutely affecting.'
Independent on Sunday

'Absolutely flawless comic writing. Original, fresh and funny.' *Observer*

'One of the best writers in the country . . . excellent, original, funny and profound.'
Daily Express

£8.99

ISBN 978 1 84767 048 9

www.canongate.tv